i

Cover design by Ibnul Affan

To Bella,

Thank you for teaching me to face my fears,

and for reminding me to always believe.

You are a blessing!

The Fantastical and Mysterious Tale

of

Sweet Pea of Monsterville:

An Interdimensional r(h)aps[odd]yssey

Within a house lived a special girl

who happened upon a secret world

Tired one night, she lay upon her bed

listening to the tale her father read

But once he finished the final words

her thoughts were mired by what she heard

A tunnel opened from her wall

A purple paw reached out to all

Seen only by true believers

she saw its claws were sharp as cleavers

Afraid, she felt she had no choice

"Don't go! The monster will get me,"

she was screaming with a pleading voice

Though her daddy tried to assuage her

alas 'twas gainst her anxious nature

Her daddy had looked all around

but there was no monster, nor a sound

Once he had sprung from off her bed,

she clung to him, and she had said,

"Don't let the monster get me! Ahhhhhhhhhhh!"

Then, gasping for air as she wheezed,

she seemed helpless, struggling to breathe

Working herself up to such a state,

she began to hyperventilate.

But her daddy had in place a plan
grasping the inhaler on her nightstand,
pumping medicine into her lungs,
stopping the attack that had begun
Her bronchioles opened; her breath returned
She was calmer and he less concerned
Upon seeing how sad she had become
he asked, "Why is it you want to run?
To your fear you must not abide
Spend not one moment trying to hide"
"Well, it's eight feet tall with yellow eyes,
a big head, long nose, and horns that rise
Its feet are under the closet door
Please don't let it scare me anymore"
Her dad wanted to see inside,
so he grabbed the doorknob and turned
Then resting his finger on his chin,
he realized a lesson she could learn
He pointed at the monster and said,
"You shall not harm one hair on her head
Monster, I'll never be scared of you
So go home to your mommy, shoo!"
What happened next was no tall order
Lo and behold, the monster was smaller
It still had scary teeth and yellow eyes
But once shrunken, she gasped in surprise

The dad had known he would not be harmed
But he still did seem quite alarmed
He stepped closer and began to shout,
"Don't think of coming here! Now get out!
Monster, you go home to your mommy!"
Alas, that's not the end of our story
It became smaller and was worried
Instead of a saunter, now it scurried
Still moving with its hot dog nose
and his teeny hamburger head,
it was now the size of a dolly
that lay on the little girl's bed
Its teeth still pointed in all directions,
but now the little girl asked a question
The creature found this all deplorable
and failing to fight 'gainst his tiny tears
it heard, "Hey, how are you this adorable?"
even with its itty-bitty ears
Wanting to speak, it had not the words, and
becoming more fearful, when 'gainst the glass
it heard the pecking of hungry birds
It was no longer a scary being
So not knowing what else to do
it decided to start screaming, "Ahhh!"
For the monster, the tension mounted
It was already too much to bear

Then the dad bent down and patted it
gently stroking its fluffy purple hair
Well that little guy became smaller still
as it stood helpless on that windowsill
The dad placed it on the palm of his hand
"What a good little monster," he said,
then added, "How's daddy's little man?"
The girl looked in her dad's palm and said,
"I'll put you between two pieces of bread
And you'll be my cute monster sandwich"
And shrinking again as she spoke those words
the little monster became more absurd
Now just a small clump of purple hair
with a head shaped like a hamburger
He said with a whisper and quite calmly
"Awh, time to go home to your mommy"
And it took her dad no time to exclaim,
"Now we blow you back from whence you came!"
Then with a whoosh, and a flick of the wrist
the teeny monster, too small to resist
had blown right out of the daddy's hand
and returned to its fantastical land
vanishing into the darkness of night
Yet within something else's sight?
Then the girl gave her dad a hug
And crawled inside the covers snug

But the girl had just one more wish

She wanted to blow the monster a kiss

So she put her hand up to her lips

And she sent a smooch with her fingertips

Well, as that little girl became older

sometimes her fear made her monsters bolder

And after she allowed them to haunt her

She remembered what her daddy taught her

She could make her monsters smaller

by placing them in the palm of her hand

and sending them to their native land

That's why the little girl used no more tears

She had finally learned how to face her fears

And so begins our epic saga

of a special girl and a tiny monster

Belief is powerful one should know
and like a seed from a dandelion
there's no telling where it will blow
It may swirl into a primordial sea
and unbeknownst to the believer
develop till its growth is complete
That tiny monster was blown to and fro
spinning tossing, turning every which way
and landed in a distant place
met by its monstrous mommy's dismay
That little girl was the Architect,
the Creator of a new world
where monsters put fright in children's hearts
and crept from the darkness unfurled
Spawning from the seed of a girl's belief
Unfolding a phantasmagorical world
which would breach, was within reach
A land with volcanoes spewing lava
where it rained globules of blood
giving mother nature its drama
A land where earthquakes shook the ground
and pounding thunder made a roaring sound
And in the distance the little monster
drifted towards its mommy's thigh

Her call was between a lion's roar

and an elephant's thunderous cry

That motherly love begot something strange

And the monster child began to change

It kept growing, and shedding its skin

to become the Prince of Terror

and a deranged leviathan

Chapter 3: A New Friend

Six years later when it's far from spring
we see the girl who would help a king
She looked out her bedroom window
as she watched all the children playing
Missing out on friendships she could sow,
her enthusiasm had been waning
The girl had asthma you can surely see
Less oxygen made her think again
She was miserable as can be
She waved to the children who played outside
But she wished she could do so much more
Her parents feared yet another attack
And much of her life was an utter bore
Of monsters she was no longer afraid
So while alone in her room
she had an idea while she played
Why do monsters have to be scary?
Why not cute, fuzzy, and well, hairy?
And this part of the story is the key
She made a friend only she could see

Chapter 4: The Wretched Brothers

In her town lived Scud and Biff Ratched
Two bullies who were drawn to weakness
like metal pulled toward a magnet
When Scud saw the girl from her window
he would let out an abrasive laugh,
being in the space of and invasive,
hurling a snowball which exploded
against the cold frost covered glass
And his brother Biff was worse or double
by taunting the girl's dog just to be mean
His actions were dark and deplorable
making it a more obscene scene
Teddy would run outside barking loudly
And Biff would bark back mockingly
pelting him with a snowball soundly
Teddy wanted to bite those bullies
He was not too keen on waiting
His front paws lay on top of the gate
showing his teeth while salivating.
The girl felt sad, but what could she do?
She was too sick to confront those boys
And she knew they would deny it too
When she saw that Scud and Biff Ratched
she knew she would one day have her druthers

getting revenge of hers on those bullies

those boys known as the Wretched Brothers

Chapter 5: Muffin Stuffins

As Scud passed underneath the enormous pink, fluorescent sign outside Muffin Stuffins it made an intermittent crackling sound. Broken sign or not, Scud was enamored with their amazing snack treats. And what was even better was that he knew how to get them for free.

He skulked out back to the dumpster, braced himself for the foul smell, opened the lid, and jumped in. Right on top of the garbage heap he found a clear plastic bag filled with an assortment of muffin holes, specialty muffins with 30 varieties of filling, and other delectable and sundriscious morsels. A day-old jelly donut had been patiently staring at him through the bag until it finally took advantage.

He walked quickly back to his house with powdered hands and lips, and a jelly-stained shirt. As he carried the bag of treats over his shoulder, wearing ripped jeans and a jacket with a broken zipper and a hole in the sleeve, he thought that he must have looked like a Santa who had fallen on hard times. But despite the beat-up clothes, his bag of pastries was something he could get excited about. He would soon cherish each one with his brother.

With a front gutter, once dangling by one bracket, stood the house of the man known as Rich Ratched. It had finally given way, and on the scraggly blades of crabgrass it stayed. The gutters that were still attached had sprouted weeds, ready to collapse.

Paint had dwindled, peeled off from the shingles, and a tree that had fallen in a storm rested along the second floor. Cracked, the concrete stairs had pieces missing, making it hard to walk without slipping. So the Wratched house was in decay, with weeds growing within the gaping gums of driveway and a septicity buried in the couch and two youths with damaged roots caused by an infected mouth.

And on that couch laid a man. with disheveled mangy hair, wearing crusty underwear, who spent his days on a mission, staring at his television. His tank top, a mixture of stains by his chest, could not contain his rounded belly, evidence of his life's zest, which raised and lowered with each breath. Here laid Rich Wratched, who had fallen asleep with a beer bottle, and his hand was still attached to it. He lived his life in a deluded and drunken fog, and the house had the smell of stale beer, cheap cigars, and wet dog, which was strange because they no longer had a dog. Scruffy, the mongrel they used to own never came back one day. Sometimes when their dad would disappear for days, the boys wondered why they stayed,

When the front door creaked open it was late, so Scud and Biff went to investigate, and they found their dad in quite a state. It was rich, seeing him on the floor snoring with a chocolate chip cookie melting slowly as it rested on his half open lips, exposing his decaying front tooth. As Biff went to put their dad's cigarette in the ashtray Scud grabbed his arm and said, "Don't help that drunken bastard. What's he ever done for you?"

He's still our dad. We can't leave him like that," said Biff, and he laid a blanket over him.

"Sometimes I think it would be better if this place burned down. Then we can finally get rid of him," said Scud. Then they both went back to sleep, wishing they had different lives.

While the girl was in her bedroom,
she started to explore in her mind
She would spend much of her time drawing
making up creatures she might find
She kept her drawings on the walls,
She placed them along the board of her bed
She had sketches of a little monster,
and over time the kingdom which he led
And she had created cities which she achieved
from different toys that she had received
The creatures there were of her own design
These were not monsters who were scary
They were the cute and fuzzy kind
The girl believed this so strongly
The drawings sparkled, shimmered, and twirled
Then outward and upward they whooshed and whirled
So this place did begin to unfold
but merging with the fearful world of old
The seeds of belief she placed on the ground
And her hopeful prayers were the soil
nurturing a world, different and profound
She brought a kingdom into existence
because of her hope, belief, and persistence
Now there were two worlds fused together

created by a child's beliefs

One based on fear, the other love

Both truths which the girl had released

Each world trying to eclipse the other

But both were ruled by only one queen

who was the monster prince's mother

Chapter 8: Sweet Pea in Monsterville

Back in the good ol' days of Monsterville, there was always fabulous weather for a little monster to play. There was of course the never-ending darkness, pelting hail, roaring and unrelenting thunder, howling wind, and bubbling lava. The monsters truly loved it, cleaning their sinuses by breathing in the steam coming from vents in the earth, taking mud baths to moisturize their fur and exfoliate their skin, and eating delectable mud pies.

But Sweet Pea was one little monster who had more than enough of what this land had to offer. He would move through the darkness slowly, shuddering throughout his little body, chattering his small dull teeth together, and wishing he was in his soft dry bed in his pinstriped pajamas. And he thought mud was slimy and full of germs, resorting to poking his muddy pattycakes with a long stick as he grimaced. He usually stayed inside the castle and looked out the window, hoping for a different life and wishing his mommy would leave him alone about being a proper monster.

This behavior was not understood by the residents of Monsterville. "Why doesn't he eat mudpies?" they all asked.

But what really made Sweet Pea stand out was the fact that he did not like scaring humans at all. And unlike all the other monsters his age, he certainly didn't brag about it. "What kind of monster doesn't scare humans?" said some, as they shook their crooked and curvy horned heads. It's absolutely ludicrous," said others as they gasped in horror.

"They never did anything to us. Why should I try to scare them?"

"Oh, how sweet," they said. "And he's so small too. Well, I bet he couldn't scare a pea. Why yes, that's what we'll call him, Sweet Pea."

"Well, I am sweet, and I don't go around hurting others," he said. "So go ahead and call me Sweet Pea. I like that name."

Then one day, for a reason unbeknownst to Sweet Pea, Monsterville began to change. He was in his usual place, looking out the window of his castle, feeling gloomy, sighing as his little paws rested against his fuzzy chin, and wondering if this was all there was to his life in a land where he knew he didn't belong. He began to wonder what it would be like if he left Monsterville for good and lived with human children. Maybe they would accept him after all. Then, just as he was about to run away, something strange happened.

Slowly, the sky became lighter. Reds, yellows, purples, and pinks appeared to be dancing above, and a golden ball began to slowly show itself moving up from the horizon. Sweet Pea was amazed, and he began to smile as he watched the most beautiful thing he had ever seen in his young life. A tear ran down his cheek, and for the first time, he felt free. Eventually, he had to avert his little eyes, for he had never seen such brightness. And meadows were filled with flowers which began to blossom. And there were fields of green. He heard the pleasant chirping sounds from the trees and saw white doves flying overhead. And there was the fluttering of butterflies, and the buzzing of bees. And while the other monsters threw down their mud pies and ran inside their caves out of fear, Sweet Pea walked outside and raised his hands towards the sky. He looked up and shouted, "Yay! What a beautiful day." And he ran through the fields, and made a crown of flowers over his head, and jumped into a nearby pond, and saw goldfish swimming in the water, and he saw a waterfall and listened to the rhythmic sound of whooshing water gently falling from the rocks. This was his greatest moment.

Chapter 9: Sweet Pea's Tale of Woe

The girl had brought the monster prince to life
Like all creatures, he had his share of strife
In the great world of Monsterville
he would be all by his lonesome
He didn't agree with monsterkind's code
and he didn't feel quite wholesome.
Picking a tulip with soft furry paws
it was colorful and smelled fresh,
and he was happy with what he saw
Then some others passed by him and said,
"Flowers are for humans if you don't mind.
Their blooming is a looming nuisance
If you love humans go live with their kind
Monsterville used to be a better place
We always slurped mud pies for breakfast
 and we had little children to chase
You couldn't scare a baby if you tried
You are the reason that we might not survive"
The youth in his world had been boastful
of how they scared human girls and boys
But the monster prince was woeful
cause being scary gave him no joy
He knew causing fear was not nice to do
And the ones who made fun of his name

taunted the monster boy for this too

All Monsterkind made him feel smothered

and most of all his monstrous mother

She wanted to strike fear in human hearts

But the little prince didn't agree

His name was Andraconous Scarititus

But he said, "You can call me Sweet Pea"

Sweet Pea gently held the crimson tulip in his hands, rubbing the smooth petals softly, as he soaked up the warmth of the sun which came through the castle window. The muscles on his back suddenly became more tense when he heard his mother call out, "Draco, where are you?" Then she added, "Come here my little monster," which she crooned in a prolonged voice that fluctuated from a heightened pitch to almost a shriek. He hurriedly tucked the flower into his little leather vest so it wouldn't be seen.

As Sweet Pea entered the queen's chamber, he saw her hard scaly tale slithering from side to side as she stood looking out her window, pondering. "Oh Draco, look at what our world has become," she said as she motioned out the window at the blooming purple cherry blossoms down below. "We can have no more of this filthy human drivel." Then she gave a rather masculine hacking cough into her sleeve, as if to clear a bad taste from her mouth.

Extending her long pointy fingers, she produced a smooth orb and, in a whisper, said, "Look deep inside my dear." And within the mysterious ball, came into view a human child in her bedroom. "This little human does not fear us," said the queen. She has changed our world. We must make her terrified again, if we are ever going to see our lovely world returned to its glory."

"But I don't like scaring humans," said Sweet Pea.

"I can't believe you talk of such things," said the queen. "You are such a disappointment," she said in a deep and foreboding voice. Sweet Pea put his head down and tried not to cry, holding back as much of a sniffle as he could. There was a pause as the queen looked out the window. "But you can change that," she said sweetly as she turned to her son from the window. "You do want to help Monsterville, don't you?"

"Yes Mommy."

"Then go to this human and bring terror into her heart," she shouted. Then our world will be restored. And you will have helped your kind."

"But I don't want to scare anyone," said Sweet Pea.

"But why not?" said the queen.

"Well, I feel a cavity coming on, and I don't want anyone to see my teeth when I snarl. So there's that..."

Then quite softly she said, "You are the Prince of Monsterville, and you will one day lead all creatures in our land. You must make sure we have a land to live in."

"Okay. I'll try, I really will. I'll do my best mommy."

"That's all I ask of you my little Draco-doodle." Then he practiced his scary face, snarling as best as he could. Then he bit his lip. "Ouch," he said, and then stubbed his toe. This was not his best day.

The girl wished as hard as she could
hoping her dream would be understood
So she said, "Monster, come out and play
Won't you please stay with me today?"
And the monster entered the girl's room
walking through a swirling passageway
His nose was damp, and his feet had claws
And instead of hands he had furry paws
His hair was golden, and his teeth were dull
Yet he had the cutest hairy mole
And covered with fuzzy shimmering strands,
he was a creature from a foreign land
Palms of periwinkle, soles of lilac,
he was scared and wanted to go back
But he still spoke despite being shy
He knew Monsterville needed him to try
"I'm Sweet Pea, monster boy of my kingdom
Please don't stare at this mole on my chin"
Trying to cause fear, he let out a roar
But much to his chagrin she said, "More, more!"
And Teddy, lying down, thought this might be
a talking rabbit he began to see
So he let out a bark and a low growl
waiting for the signal to chow down

The drool from his snout splattered 'gainst the floor
But Isabella just told him to stay
as she ran out her room and closed the door
She was excited to tell her daddy
who spent time alone with his dusty books
yet would be pleased to see her happy
"Dad, I created a monster," she said
"That's great," was his simple reply
buried deeply in the pages he read
He knew she spent a lot of time alone
"Pretending is fun, isn't it?" he said
in both a smug and playful tone
"Sweetheart, please go back to your room and play
 I need to finish my work today"
"Stay with me daddy and see my monster
He's as cute as a little button
Please, before he decides to wander"
So he went to his little girl's room
And with the pretend monster he did play
But her dad didn't see anything
since Sweet Pea kept himself far away
Teddy put his front paws on the window
He whimpered and lay down with sad eyes
Then the monster emerged from the vortex
Once again to Isabella's surprise
"Are you looking for me?" said Sweet Pea

"I don't want just anyone to see"

Then he became sad, and started to cry

"No one is scared of me; I don't know why"

"I know you can't hurt me," said the girl,

"Monsters don't really exist in the world"

Although they were her infatuation

They were just from her imagination

"So stop that crying, and let's be friends.

This sadness needs to come to an end"

Then Sweet Pea looked around the girl's room

And what he saw raised some questions

for which he wanted answered soon

 Colorful drawings were on the walls some

And he noticed a quite peculiar one

It was himself that he did indeed see

"But how can you have this picture of me?"

Before her answer, he looked at the others

And he saw his furry footed mother

"How can this be?" said the monster prince

"Have you seen my world?" he asked as he winced

"I think you are being somewhat crazy

Unless my wishes have come true, maybe?"

The little prince did continue to speak some

"What's your name? From what kingdom do you

come?"

"I'm Isabella, and I'm from no kingdom.

I live in Maplewood New Jersey,

which is a place filled with wisdom"

"All right Isabella of New Jersey

What is this beast before me that I see?

It looks like no monster known to me"

When Teddy growled and showed his incisors,

the monster trembled and spoke more wisely

If Teddy finds your face to be kind

he will be loyal till the end of time

The monster knew not how those drawings appeared

But there's another matter which had reared

"Monsters like scaring others," said Sweet Pea

"Causing fear has a rich history

But some don't believe in monsters anymore

And our world has become rather ugly"

Then the girl's jaw dropped onto the floor

And the monster prince smirked quite smugly

"If you're not afraid, I'll be in trouble,

Please don't send me back having failed

Come meet the Queen with me on the double

Tell her I scared you and took you to our world

And then I'll be a hero to all

The girl did want to have an adventure

So she agreed to go with the monster

even though she had just met him

 "Take me to your mommy," said the girl

"I can be of help in the monster world"

Chapter 12: The Queen of Monsterville

So Sweet Pea, Teddy, and Isabella
went through the portal in the bedroom wall,
And quickly did they enter the kingdom,
where all monsters, both big and small
discovered where the monster prince had been
The girl admired this land's beauty
the rainbows, shining sun and gentle breeze
yet was befuddled by a golden patootie
lying beyond the cotton candy trees
The creatures who dwelled here seemed troubled
And this world was beheld as a monstrosity
They all blamed it on little Sweet Pea
for his complete lack of ferocity
But now they all saw Isabella,
hoping her fear would make their world better
Some foul, scowling and growling from the crowd,
Others unwound their snouts on the ground
revealing how they were endowed,
and made a loud trumpeting sound
Sweet Pea lied, his world he tried to despise
But the guise was not a surprise,
for those with paws, claws, and googly eyes
He turned to the girl whom he had brought here
And tried to show her some sense

He wanted to please his sour faced mommy
to avoid a day of recompense
"I miss the glory days," said that little guy,
"When we had rain clouds, mud and grey skies"
He started to become kind of weepy
These grasses and flowers, are plain creepy"
Then far off in the distance she flew in
The Monster Queen from the Black Lagoon
She had quite a bit of assistance
never needing to even use a spoon.
Her breath smelled of rotting sweet potato,
and her snaggletooth gave her a lisp
She turned to the little girl and said,
"Darling, won't you please give us a kiss?"
Her horns were raised like a rhinoceros
She had a face of a long-nosed monkey
She donned spurs on her lizard skin boots,
and they made a sound that was clunky
The queen knew she must make this girl afraid,
for children should not control their fears
Flowers and sunshine were the price they paid
And she needed Sweet Pea to bring her here.
"There is a task which you must undertake
A proposition for you my sweet
You must complete it, for your family's sake,
If you wish to suckle from freedom's teat

For if you ever plan to leave this land

You must face my eldest child,

the Leviathan, a monster big and grand"

And now the little girl was worried,

for she didn't know what awaited.

She came here to help the monster prince

But felt nervous from what the queen stated.

Teddy whimpered and stayed close to his master

And Sweet Pea looked somewhat concerned

The girl thought, Did I cause this disaster?

I thought I was helping these creatures

My how the situation had turned.

Then the queen took the girl to a portal,

and told her to do what she must

She knew the beast would fill the girl with fear,

in that wonderful idea she did trust

But Sweet Pea was grateful to have a friend

And he didn't want this girl's life to end

So, wanting to help, he gave Isabella a sword

Now, she finally had a weapon

a sharp blade which could not be ignored

She accepted it graciously for she did not know,

how she would defeat this beast in the portal below

The portal opened on the other side,

and Isabella stared at a beast,

 a slithering creature 3 feet wide

The shadows in the darkened room

were only somewhat revealing

of this monster with a head on the wall

and a body clinging to the ceiling

And at the corners, each curled up in a ball

two boys cowered with nowhere to crawl

Terror could be seen on each boy's face

One was ghostly white with a maggot's writhe

the other frozen in place, petrified

And who they were was equally tragic

Lo and behold, it was Scud and Biff Ratched

The little girl held the sword's handle

with the blade still sheathed in its scabbard,

and she said, "M-m-m-monster be gone,"

 as she stood, shivered, and stammered

But the menacing creature would not stop

It just slithered toward her and licked its chops

The girl trembled, and her arms did shake,

taking a few steps back, for goodness' sake

The beast hissed and continued to advance

And the girl almost made in her underpants

This creature was truly a beast of terror
which struck her with fear and made her tremble
With eyes closed she swung at the winged beast,
blood spattering and sizzling on the floor,
Then it quivered, twitched, and contorted,
all according to Monsterville lore
Smoke appeared as it began to melt almost to nothin'
the girl with the sword said, "Ain't that somethin"
Meanwhile in the land of Monsterville
candy cane trees changed to scraggly branches
because fear from this little girl's heart
 provided ugliness with more chances
to rear its head and rise from the earth
This world was still the monster queen's turf
 And that big momma knew she had won,
for she had given the girl the right test
The sprouting of fear's seed had begun
She saw the girl had failed, cheering "Yes, yes!"
Suddenly from the smoke a creature formed
For the girl's fear made the beast reborn
She knew she still needed to be concerned
cause within seconds this beast had now returned
Except the Leviathan was larger
and had not one but three beastly heads,
and the girl was filled with enormous dread

Isabella now cowered as the Leviathan stood over her, with sharp horns protruding from each head. Each had three different faces, one in the front, and one on each side. The front was that of a dragon, which starred with cold unblinking eyes. The left side resembled a hawk with an open beak ready to clasp down, and on the right resembled a lion, which revealed sharp teeth as it roared. Each head connected to a long scaly neck. And all the necks were attached to a large body covered with plates like a dinosaur down its spine, all except the wings, which were that of an eagle.

The middle head breathed heavily, the steam from its nostrils blowing back Isabella's hair as it let out a screech like a condor which had the sound of nails against a chalkboard, making her spine shiver. And some strands of mucus blew out onto her clothes and on the floor.

Isabella looked at Sweet Pea in disbelief. "How could you do this to me?" she said. "You were supposed to be my friend."

As Sweet Pea looked away, he saw the blooming cherry blossoms begin to shrivel, and he knew he had made a terrible mistake. He once again took out the crimson tulip from his vest pocket and gently rubbed the petals as he watched Isabella fight the Leviathan. He saw the petals wither as he looked down at them, and then he felt how they crunched in his palm. This is not what he wanted for Monsterville, and it's not what he wanted for Isabella. Sweat began to form beads against his forehead, as he saw the girl who loved him struggle to survive. He knew this was all happening because he brought Isabella to Monsterville. Why couldn't he have just told her to stay in her world?

Then the Mommy Monster Queen looked at Sweet Pea and said, "Well, you brought this human here. So I suppose we owe this all to you. Isn't that right Sweet Pea?" which she said mockingly. "You will be my legacy Andraconous. You will inherit this kingdom, and you will be the ruler that Monsterville needs. Suddenly, a crown of brambles grew on Sweet Pea's head, and as the thorns sunk into his fur, he let out a shriek of agony. He tried to rip them off, but they just sunk deeper. He felt quite sad and hung his head downwards.

He had always gone along with what he had been told about the way of monsterkind. But he knew he could no longer try to do things the monster way. He needed to do things the Sweet Pea way.

Suddenly, he grabbed hold of Teddy, and climbed onto his back, and with a loud, "Kiah," they jumped through the portal

42

So the little prince was in a state
as he watched from the portal's other side
He regretted the decision he had made
and being angry at his mommy
jumped through on Teddy, taking a ride
He had done what his mommy told him
Now he witnessed the impossible
He wanted to protect the little girl
 And he felt utterly responsible
Teddy pounced on the thick scaly head,
and Sweet Pea let out a monstrous roar
It was directed at his own kind,
which right now he rightly did abhor
The Leviathan shook off these creatures
and its claw pinned Sweet Pea on the ground
One head in front of the monster prince
another by the girl, ready to pounce
Teddy hit the wall, whimpered, and yelped
And the girl saw that her dog needed help
She became anxious and struggled to breathe,
shaking as she wiped the sweat from her sleeve
reaching for her inhaler as she wheezed,
but the beast whipped his long scaly tail,
knocking it from her trembling hands

For he knew the seed of fear, when watered
will grow and exponentially expand
So searching for her pump whilst on her knees
she heard her heart thump faster and louder
thinking of the mommy monster queen,
wondering, "Should I bow to her?"
Then, she felt a voice coming from inside,
one she trusted which soothed her when she cried
She remembered her dad's words from long ago,
and his advice, which she happened to know
This beast was merely her imagination,
She knew he was of her own creation
dropping her sword with no lack of drama,
shouting "Beast be gone, go back to your momma!"
Next thing she knew there was a whish and a whoosh,
with yelping followed by its scaly tush.
Then the beast slithered through the portal
And this scene became a lot less awful
The monster's retreat did seem to calm her
Lo and behold, it returned to its momma
With the monster gone it was quiet
as Sweet Pea lay still upon the ground
Isabella drew near him in silence
his heart though big, no longer made a sound
Teddy whimpered and licked his furry face,
but no sign of life, not even a trace

Oh the prince gave his life to save a friend

having fought valiantly with the beast

so the reign of terror would end

Sweet Pea was a gallant warrior

whose sacrifice made the fearmonger cease

The scene couldn't have been gorier

for a gentle soul, our Prince of Peace

His bones were crushed, his spleen was shattered

His head was bloodied, his fur was tattered

Lifeless, he laid there, his soul now gone

"Nooo," Isabella said. "This is all wrong"

She held the monster boy in her arms

and shed a tear for the little monster

who put himself in the way of harm

She loved that monster boy, and he loved her,

And love's power is not to be deterred

So she took Sweet Pea to his mommy

And all of Monsterkind bared witness

The mood was solemn, the day was balmy

And all the monsters felt listless

So wanting to say a proper farewell

they went back through the strange portal

Now the monsters all gathered round

They viewed the prince's lifeless body

And for a time, no one made a sound

As the girl's tear dropped on Sweet Pea's nose

Isabella noticed it she supposed
It was a mixture of love and belief
And she could sense something stirring
something which lay hidden beneath
Slowly Sweet Pea opened his eyes,
and then he took in a deep breath
He was happy the girl was with him
and happy she had avoided death
Within the space of merely hours
his crown of brambles had budded flowers
And now that they returned to Monsterville,
they discovered a land more beautiful
The water was clear, and fish could be seen
Who could believe their world was serene?
“Thank you for saving us,” said Biff and Scud
“I can’t believe that really happened
We see that monster in our dreams at night
And the idea of escape for us
well, it was an idea we had abandoned
We won’t bother you again,” they told her
 And they both sincerely meant it
“We like it much better in this world
 And our home, well we want to forget it”
 “I am glad I could help,” said Isabella
“And I really didn’t have a choice
It was the monster living in our minds

which we all had given a voice"
Then Isabella turned confidently
and she spoke to the Mommy Monster Queen
She had come to know things from what she had seen
"Believe in yourselves; life will get better
Trading in fear, leaves each creature a debtor
Make peace instead of being scary
Be loving and don't be contrary
You are beautiful beings in this world
accept who you are, you'll feel love for all,
including of course this little girl"
Well the queen had given the girl her best,
but couldn't deny, the girl made some sense
And amongst all of the monsters,
 there was not an ounce of resentment,
for after the saving of Sweet Pea
they were all touched by her sentiments
Then a manticore came forth
 amidst the cacophonous crowd,
and repeated the word, "Dangalingus"
which began softly as a whisper
 yet gradually became quite loud
Others joined in, chanting in unison
Suddenly the bloated bowels amongst
the hideous horde began to loosen
Their enthused shouts became still louder,

when she hoped they would be waning

And Isabella looked at Sweet Pea,

concerned about what the monsters were saying

"They believe the savior has appeared

who brought me back with a single tear"

Isabella said, "Excuse me, monsters

But I have something important to say

I'm no Dangalingus, no friggin way"

The monsters were shocked at her statement

For this was all contrary to lore

Then suddenly the octoblob plopped

 making a jelly-like mess on the floor

It was a hot mess with googly eyes

a creature which just came into being

And it opened its mouth in surprise,

shocked and dismayed by what it was seeing

It tried to pull itself together

Indeed it wanted to throw a fit

But it just gesticulated

with its steaming gelatinousness

And let out the words, "Oh, shit"

The misease of this faeces

 was an entirely new species,

and when it spoke and it stank,

the creatures' hearts' sank

Having been shocked into silence,

The monsters were no longer musical,
And the mutatious golden eyed shoofly
 regurgitated his squirrelcicle
But then the creatures of Monsterville
had begun to shout, chant and cheer
For they knew this girl would do great things here
So they ranted well into the night
quite sure of her destined and foretold plight
And so it happened, though quite unexpected,
scaring humans had become
what the creatures rejected
Meanwhile, the Mommy Monster Queen
found herself looking at a golden sun
She was also in shock by what happened
and needed to ponder what should be done
Monsterville is a land that had changed,
and the queen had much to consider
The Leviathan had been tamed,
but would it help if she were bitter?
She needed a plan of how to proceed
based on everything that had occurred
and considering what Monsterville needs
She motioned for quiet amongst the crowd
 Then said, "You have bested my champion,
and for that feat you should be proud
Come, let's rest now that you have returned

and embrace a future I had once spurned

Stay with us and sleep in my castle

I'll decide what should be done about you

Chapter 16: The Beastly Knave

The beastly knave

had slithered to its cave,

 still determined to prevail

The world it knew

was no longer true

So it slumped and dragged its tail

Within its lair,

the beast did stare

in a bucket of bubbling water

then dropped its jaw

from what it saw

Yet the mission, it would not abort her

It had seen

a gruesome scene

 which made it feel quite queasy

and was balmy,

 upon watching its mommy

So it decided on something sleazy

Chapter 17: The Leviathan Strikes Back

The beast needed to speak to its mommy
Since it was unsure of her intentions
The thought of monsters befriending humans
This would require an intervention
So it went to the queen's castle
flying through the darkness of the night
It had done quite a bit of scheming,
so it could do what it believed was right
The queen told it of her desire
To begin a totally new era
So monsters can be loving to humans,
and their worlds can be made better
"Whom Sweet Pea loves, I have tried to destroy,
Oh, how I have wronged my sweet monster boy
At sunrise I will announce my plan
 that will be enacted throughout this land
It's one for which my boy has been wishin
and for which the monsters have been itchin"
The beast was angry and disappointed
that the monster queen changed her belief
It needed to get ahead of this,
or at the very least underneath
"Mom, this is not how you raised me to be
You must have one of your tentacles

writhing up your maggot laden sleeve"
And so the impetus for the willingness
to be villainous was imminent
From infancy to infamy,
now brilliantly within close proximity,
it used its malignancy
to bring forth its ascendancy
So the Leviathan hugged its mommy
holding her close and quite tightly
And the next thing that happened
was rather obscene, and downright unsightly,
It had pulled its mommy deep within
for she could not resist her son.
And where the two had formerly stood,
now there was a mass of only one
So its plan was beginning to happen
It needed to be the Big Kahuna
the one who would be Monsterville's captain

"Hello, my monstrosity of a mutha," said the beast.

"Oh, how you flatter me, my number one son. Come here my little beastie boo. Kissy, kissy. Muh, Muh. Oh, you have some schmutz on your cheek."
The beast looked at the queen stoically and said, "If I can slowly drain the lives of helpless bunnies and puppies, I can certainly clean my own face."

"Yes, you certainly are a big boy. But you must have missed a spot," she said, as she took a doily, wiped it on her long slithery tongue, and smeared the beast's face with it. "There, I got it."

"Oh, come on mom, not in front of my friends."

"Okay, my little cookie. Let's talk privately if that is what you wish." But seriously, we need to discuss a most pressing matter."

"So, is it true?" the beast said. Have yooze given up on everything ya tawght me?

"Oh my three headed slithering little bloodsucking baby, you need not worry one tiny porous protrusion on your jiggly neck flesh, for tomorrow will be a day steeped in glory! I will announce that monsters change their ways. The little human girl is right. We can be loving to these creatures and make our world a better place."

"Is there anything this goombah can say to help you change your mind?"

"Nope," she said. Then she paused. "This is the new monster way. And with your help, it will be grand."

"I know yooze the queen and all, but that just ain't gonna happen."

"Look here my little beastie, don't you bite the claw that feeds you." said the queen rather forcefully.

The beast said, "Mommy, for all intensive purposes, I'm heah to stop yooze from doin what you gotta do." Then the Leviathan grabbed the Mommy Monster Queen and squeezed, absorbing her, until what was left was a crazed Leviaquesha.

The queen struggled to push out the beast. Her head bulged, and the features of one of the beast's heads started to come out. But the Leviathan said, "Hey chief! What a you kiddin? You can't get rid ah me," and pushed the protrusion back down. Then the beast said, "Boom! Done!"

Chapter 18: A Crazed Leviaquesha

The queen called an important meeting
since the knave knew her plan would need impeding
Monsters excreting, who drooled while eating
Sure, some of them must a been disgusting
But were they feared? And was it fleeting?
"Fellow monsters, I have the solution
It's plain, a campaign to bring mud and rain
and strike fear in the hearts of humans,
so we make our homeland great again
Put away those smiles and show our rage
We can't be friendly in this day and age
Monsters are scary and the world must see
We must accept who we're destined to be
So we must all spread fear throughout the world
Show the dungeon to this troublesome girl
Sweet Pea, what a disappointment you've become
Choosing this human over your own kind,
you're a traitor and no longer my son
Now we must live in this horrible world
for which you are solely responsible
I never thought that such selfish acts
for a monster could be possible
So you will join your human in a pit
filled with both of your own discontent

There you'll suffer each moment you spend
Then we'll cut off your troublesome head
and place it on a pike near the castle
You will pay for what you have done,
you abhorrent little rascal"
Then down Sweet Pea's furry cheek
ran a torrent of salty tears
deprived of the treasure he did seek,
she had confirmed his greatest fear
All this time, he had wanted to be
nurtured by a sweet loving momma
This tirade she made, with a migraine he paid
and left him feeling sorta sombre
Then somethin' strange started happenin'
to this monster lovin' mutha
Her neck had rolled, then her head did bulge
like a pink bubbled Hubba Bubba
Soon her luminous protuberance
grew smaller and smoother and
her head's shape snapped back into place
Her stuporous shouts were numerous
"Help me," she said, reaching for his embrace
"This beast I raised is inside me
 and up till now it's been hidden
Take this stake and run it through my heart
And within minutes of your assistance,

you'll bid this evil good riddance
It must be that Monsterville is free
of this darkness which is inside
There's no other way for victory today
It is an evil which must be denied"
All the monsters heard what she sayd
and couldn't abstain from the tearful cascade
But the monster prince wiped his salty tears,
for it was not a time to cry
He had to sacrifice his mommy
so that scaley Leviathan would die
Then Sweet Pea stabbed the monster queen
through the plated scales of her chest
Needing to save Monsterville from evil,
it was a difficult deed, but it was best
The queen had fallen, and her blood spattered
onto the fair prince's fur and shoes
He was in shock at what he had witnessed,
not knowing what else he could do
Then he kneeled amidst raucous silence,
nauseated from what he had done
He was not able to forgive himself,
since his mother was killed by her son
The little guy had strict morals
by which he had always been bound
And now, not sure if he was free or broken,

he threw his saber onto the ground

Then from the queen's nose and mouth

the Leviathan's essence was revealed

And the winged beast took flight,

no longer having her as a monstrous shield

Then the queen spoke as she lay on the grass,

raising her monstrous monkey head,

Thinking that each strained breath could be her last

She knew she'd pass from life to death

"Oh, my sweet little Dracodoodle,

I know this monster has been tough,

It was crucial you have my approval

I should have loved you for who you are

Oh, I was so loathsome and gruff

I am sorry that what you valued, I tried to destroy

You'll always be my sweet little monster boy

So don't be sad about what you have done

You have saved our beloved Monsterville,

and I am proud you are my son"

And with those words the queen did collapse

fatally scathed from the beast's artful trap

The queen's disdain had returned with pain

Yet she changed at the end of her fearful reign

And where she had lain, she would remain

Her tongue no longer slithered

Her temples no longer pulsed

Her cowboy boots were still smoking,

from the pull of her parasitic host

Alas, the queen of the monsters was slain

And the prince was alone in the world again

62

Oh that Sweet Pea knew the beast shall rue
for it was a creature he did abhor
He vowed to rend, so his heart could mend
and avenge his mommy evermore
Despite his grief, from what laid beneath,
tomorrow would be a day anew
And when Sweet Pea spoke, he did hope invoke,
because the aim of his words was true
"Monsters, for the queen's soul we should pray
She sacrificed and atoned for her sins
 That mommy changed the monster way."
The monsters stopped as Sweet Pea spoke
And they were all listening for more
Sweet Pea trusted the little guy within,
and his words carried a thunderous roar
"We all know, it's time to make a change,
We can't be bullies in this day and age
We have to accept who we've become,
We can love others, and love ourselves some
Let us show humans how to make peace
with what in their minds they are seeing
The fear which bound us is actually freeing
 Let us all unite, in acceptance of this new world
And bestow an honor on this special girl

Isabella of Maplewood,

You are the Savior of all Monsterkind

a knight of peace, using the power of your mind

Thank you for uniting monsters and humans

Without your help we would not know

what it is we should be doing

Once again, the passageway opened,

matter unwoven to return to the world of men

The new savior entered the portal

She had helped a king, though a mere mortal

 Having the hearts of all monsterkind mended

Her journey to that foreign land had ended

And so concludes another chapter in our epic saga,

of a little girl and an even smaller monster

Isabella awoke in her bed
Her thinking lingering, eyes twinkling
with an inkling of the craziest dream
An illusion, or could it be proven?
Had her mind arranged some deranged scheme?
Then she heard Teddy yelp, whine, and whimper
So soothing words in his ear she whispered
Yet she noticed when she gave him a hug
golden strands of fur on her rug
That seemed strange, something was awry
Might it explain that cute little guy?
Monsterville was incredible and real
She ran with zeal, to reveal her ordeal,
her creation from clay on her potter's wheel
But her dad crumbled and stumbled
for he couldn't conceal his Achilles heel
She went downstairs, Teddy following along
And she saw her dad who had been forlorn
"Isabella my precious girl,
 you've been missing for six days," he cried.
"I have been worried sick about you"
and she looked quite surprised
"Six days gone, but how could that be?"
It felt like a few hours since she

went through the passageway with Sweet Pea

She told him of the monster prince

and the adventure they had

But the more she explained

the more he thought she had gone mad

"Who is this Sweet Pea?" he wanted to know

"Why, he's the prince of all the monsters

He needed help, and he begged me to go"

Her dad didn't have a clue what to say,

except to shake his head in dismay

He didn't believe monsters existed

A fact, he wholeheartedly resisted

Spending time in her room by herself

must have affected her mental health

Those drawings in her room had become

a very unhealthy obsession.

Bringing her to a psychiatrist

about her highly unstable mind,

making an emergency appointment

 with the most renowned expert he could find

And as she sat there in the waiting room,

Sweet Pea arrived not a moment too soon

Her dad sat in the soft leather chair of the chief resident's office of Crestfallen Falls Psychiatric Hospital with an unshaven face, dark sunken bags under his eyes, and hair still unbrushed after waking up on the living room sofa.

He spoke to the man in the white lab coat, as he mumbled frantically, with his back hunched over and his palms against his face. "I just don't know what is wrong with my sweet Isabella," he said. "She always had an active imagination from the time she was very little. Like other children, she was afraid of monsters under her bed, and in the closet. But now she has become completely delusional," he said, shaking his head. "I have been worried sick about her. Disappearing for almost a week without a note or anything!"

His forehead was clammy, and beads of sweat began to run down the divot of his spine. "Then she turns up, and tells us such an outlandish story about where she has been."

"Yes, what did she tell you Mr. de la Fleur?" It's okay, we are here to help, said the doctor."

"She has convinced herself that she has been helping some creature in, would you believe it -- a place called Monsterville. How can she be so removed from reality? She could have been killed wondering around outside."

"I'll talk with her Mr. de la Fleur," said the doctor as he checked off various categories on a chart and took notes on his clipboard. "We can certainly hold her for observation, but you need to sign these forms."

"I'll sign whatever I need to. I just want my daughter back." The doctor took out a folder and pulled out a legal sized carbon copy form.

"Just fill these out, and we'll do our best to help her. You do understand that these things can take some time before they get better, don't you?"

"Please do what you can."

"We will. Now let's admit her." the doctor pressed the large red glowing buzzer on his desk which shone brightly, and almost immediately, there were loud footsteps which drew closer. As they both walked out to the waiting room, an enormous intern with a shaved head that rested on top of a thick neck and broad shoulders appeared with a large needle that glistened from the light above. As he held it up, he smirked.

"I don't think we will be needing that quite yet Demetrious," said the doctor. And must you always be so dramatic?" The intern, looking disappointed, pouted, his lower lip jutting out as he put down the needle.

Chapter 22: The Coronation of Sweet Pea

In the monster world there passed some time

And life was going well for Monsterkind

The little prince did one day become king,

And on his day of coronation,

There did a peculiar event bring

All of Monsterville was present

and every creature was quite content

They had all awaited a long time

to witness the monster boy's assent

There was the finest food in all the land

with glazed centipede and unsweetened sand

The upside-down spider egg cake

was delightfully delectable

While the steamed mucus de jour

was a meal, solid yet flexible

But the broiled jellyfish soup stole the night

Its star, the nephew of the mayor,

was a lovably monstrous parasite

All the creatures were looking happy

and Sweet Pea was deemed Big Monster Pappy.

Then Monstropritees was on the Mic

the master of monster hip hop

who pulled up with his monstercycle,

which was quite a peculiar sight

the zombified thumb strutted its stuff
And sluggo left a gooey trail
The millinezilla reared its ugly head
And uncoiled its feathery tail
As the globe-asaurus floated above
It's bioluminescence lit the floor
And the hangry gi-normo-rabbit[1]
gnawed on his prickly wicker chair
While the melodiponomous
let out a bottomless roar
A squirrelonomous[2] heard the sound
He was happy for the little king
He started throwing his nuts around
and wondered what this leadership would bring
It was because of his pointy teeth
that blood trickled as he sucked his thumb
Oh, if he knew the future he would seethe
but he did not know what was to come
Part humorous, yet part ominous
as he foamed profusely from his mouth,
Meanwhile the blobaponomous,
keen on slugo, shifted his mind south
The Tyranno-trumposaurus[3]
was the only creature in dismay
roaring to all but with nothing to say,
a bully who used his writhing tongue,

to make a mockery of the land,

as he held one of his prized kitties

which he grabbed with his little baby hands

donning a deranged vampiric squid

where a typical monster's hair should be,

jamming its blood funnel into his skull

which added to his monstrosity

He was still angry with monsterkind

For he wasn't chosen to be king

The monsters knew his gigantic ego

would soon a disastrous day bring

Then he grabbed a fluffy kitten

since respect was something he was missin'

Being rich, he did what he could afford

He liked it better than to be ignored

He said, "I can do it, cause I'm famous

If you don't agree, you're an ignoramus"

He was braggadocious about his brain

And his behavior was atrocious,

wanting to keep humans from coming in

"Sweet Pea will leave Monsterville in ruins

Was he even born in our world?

How do we know he's not really human?"

The monsters who heard this began to shout,

"Hey Sweet Pea, please show this monster out

We thinks that everyone is quite perturbed

Show this dastardly dude that he's disturbed"

Chapter 23: The Epic Rap Battle of Sweet Pea and Tyranno-trumposaurus

Narrator:

So Sweet Pea jumped on stage, taking the mic
and busted some rhymes to end the night
And it all sounded something like this:

Sweet Pea:

My name is Sweet Pea, ruler of these lands
My sweet candy melts in your mouth, not hands
My mommy always said, 'Son don't tattle'
For 5 years I played with my rattle
But now I am a monsta who's prosperous
who wantsta destroy the preposterous
and ready for this epic rap battle

Tyranno-trumposaurus:

I done a told ya, your fear's my soldier
I spread terror like Ebola
My BAM and THWAP will knock out ya moula.
Cause I'm like Mr. Myagi
And your sweetness just can't top me...
I show your moms the phenoms of my crane
So she just can't drop me

*(He gets on one leg and extends his arms at his sides,
ready to do a crane kick. There are a bunch of Ohhs
from the crowd.)*

Creature from Audience:

Did you just hear what that dude said about Sweet
Pea's mamma?

Tyranno-trumposaurus:

I'm like Inigo Montoya,

a smooth swashbucklin destroya [1]

Sweet Pea:

Your beastin's all out of orda,

All the monstas ignore ya

Your wig's squishy and mushy

You can't be an incensed Übermensch

and have an octopus for a pussy

*(Tyranno-Trumposaurus stops stroking the vampire
squid on his head and grimaces. The vampire squid
meows, then hisses.)*

Partygoers:

Oh snap, I heard that

Tyranno-trumposaurus:

I'm the splendiferous O.G.

like Obi-Wan Kenobi

One pass of my lightsaber

and your mom more than knows me

Kwishuuuuuuuuuu!

Sweet Pea:

You don't scare me; I know what's right

You're like Ming the Merciless

And I'm Flash Gordon

Gonna rock-it to your moms

Till four in the mornin [2]

I'm sweet like a pea, and boy I'm able...

Tyranno-trumposaurus:

But you're too small, to sit at a table

Now me, I want to change the world...

Sweet Pea:

But your belief's just a fable

You got an L on your bald head

And it's the worst kind of label

(Holding up his left hand and forming an L on his forehead)

Party Goers:

You go Sweet Pea!

(And they all held up their hands over their heads and formed an L, and made their lips form the word for

Sweet Pea:

Okay, now it's my turn

You're a trump-posterous narcissist

A societal arsonist

with a deranged hypothesis

I won't pardon this, cause you can't resist

using words that are childish

You're a cancerous cyst that is gaping

a cantankerous master of forsaking

oozing cacophonous puss, just taking

You smile and try to beguile

You're a divisive crocodile

who's an elderly child

And no matter what you acquire

or how many creatures you fire,

you have tiny trumpcated hands,

And your face is orange, not tan

But not me; I'm the original monstrosity - O.M.

I'm a perfect living poe-em

Over the world I roe-em

I've got soft fur, but you need a co-e-mb

We don't want your trumped-up golden showers

trickling down on our hopeful heads

You'll overflow the swamp, not drain it I bet

We don't want aboundingly loud bites of sound

You think you're entitled to this crown

But you'd just bring down this monstrous town

So here's what I wish fah

Leave not with a bang, but a whimpah

Narrator:

But suddenly there was a rumble

along with a loud high-pitched sound

Like the trumpets and stomps of elephants

which made everyone look around

Then where the Eastern Mountains should be,

was darkness as far as their eyes could see

The celebration had been ruined
And it had ended quite abruptly,
For the monsters stood with open jaws
in shock from the void in their country
Many were afraid, and all were confused
And no one seemed to know what to do
The ginormapede was cut off
And the bewilderbeast, scratched his brow
There could be no denying
a panic had set in amongst the crowd
Then a monster spoke who would not be shushed
It was a transbioluminescent
Octo-blob-ity-blob-i-pus
Who opened its peculiar beak to speak
 about the chaotic cacophony
When the women monsters tried to stop him
he said, "Yo, get these muthas offa me.
Chewpacabra was shocked and spit out his gum,
the giant sloth stepped on the gooey mess
and then in slow motion began to run
Sasquatch, terrified was all out of sass
The manticore almost choked on its corn
and feeling dirty, took a bath.
Barf Fader wheezed, gasping for breath,

And the mummy was tongue tied as can be,

The Loch Ness monster called for his mommy,

As he climbed and then hid up a tree.

The Jabberwocky had nothing to say,

While Clownicula[1] who had a frown,

could only try to mime his dismay.

The centaurs were two times twice behooved

And the whimsically musical

 indefatigably magical

 and highly incompatible

 testicle had to be subdued

Rolling into the woods he tried to hide

But that monster due put on his robe,

For he could not abide

Then the voluminous and luminous

uterus cowered in the dark from fear

while the googly eyed gobbledegook-y-pus

looked for his missing humerus

and having lost all hope, couldn't grab a beer

The harangoutang sang sadly in the rain

claiming it couldn't take the pain

driven insane, ashamed, feeling lame

Meanwhile the melodiponomous

wretched malodorous vomitus

as the octolupagus having too much of this

 crawled into his sarcophagus,

since there was no stoppin this

The diabolical and maniacal

chocodiacle fled on his bicycle

Then the polka dotted pajamanosorous

Fearfully dropped all of its dots

And the frogadactyl's bloated belly

turned yellow and let out whimpering rib-botz

Even the Tyranno-trumposaurus

was fatigued, and he needed to sit

This was a mystery, big league

So he was a little less full of it

"I will build a casino and restore the Eastern

Mountains to their former glory. Trumposaurus!"

And with that, the blob plopped,

The Kraken clanged,

Scarecrow cackled,

Cyclops cried,

Grendel grunted,

The frost giant fainted,

Skilletor[2] dinged,

Smelliosis passed gas,

Humpty watched,

Dumpty swallowed [4]

the ear troll waxed on,

and the mutatious fly

regurgitated his squirrelcicle[3]

But the monster king had an idea
He would find Isabella of Maplewood
to help him get his thinking clear

As he went through the portal between worlds,
Sweet Pea knew of the danger that loomed
Donning pinstriped pants that were adorable,
he appeared in the doctor's waiting room
Upon seeing the little monster king,
Teddy wagged his tail, slobbered and drooled
And taken aback by the animal's glee
Sweet Pea knew he had not been a fool
"I'm happy to see you too Teddy,"
he said with no grandiosity
Then he wiped the slobber off of him
and told the savior the atrocity
"There is a wise troll who lives in the North
in the mountains of our majestic land
He's a seer and enlightened being
whose quintessence shines like a diamond
His beautiful melodies are sweet
And his voice will provide the answers
So we better start mountain climin'
if we want to learn from a master"
And so they both began their journey
to the top of the Northern Mountains
Both of them eager to discover
the mystery of nothingness which happened

They walked through a meadow of flowers

With an abundance that were in bloom.

Their happiness would soon be devoured

"We will be there in no time," said Sweet Pea

 But the king had spoken much too soon

They viewed stupendously sized tulips

and daisies which seemed to dance with the breeze,

They were struck by the sweet smell of jasmine

and wisterias brushed against their sleeves

Clematis Tangutica was there

with its fluffy seeded heads,

patiently waiting with twining tendrils

to find its mark, latch on, and imbed

There was the buzzing of honeybees

and the dancing leaves of willow trees

And then something from below suddenly,

the king felt trying to get cuddly

A vine had wrapped itself up Sweet Pea's leg

It writhed slowly without much of a sound

And pulled him towards the earth

trying to bring him into the ground

A wisteria made its way to Teddy,

entangling its cord around his snout

The plants gave them no second chances,

and would not let the three heroes out

And Isabella struck with her sword,

trying to protect those whom she loved

But the more she hacked the more they attacked,

now coming down from above

Then one of the vines held onto her blade

and pulled it far away

Man, that vegetation was alive

and voicing its dismay

Then a sweet melody flowed from a flute

and those tendrils loosened and swayed

And the little faun kept playing

as they skipped and twirled away

They were monsters of the jungle

of whom Sweet Pea had only heard rumors

Their heads had horns; their legs had hooves

And one donned purple polka dotted bloomers

The fauns did not want to be scary

And had not agreed with Monsterkind

So they made their way to the jungle

to a place they hoped no one would find

Soon the plants loosened their stranglehold

As the sound of lyres joined the melody

Two humans strummed, untangling marigolds

And that was all Isabella's eyes did see

"Thanks for your help," said Isabella. "But who are you? And how did you get here?" Teddy went over to the men, whining and wagging his tail, and began licking them. "And why is my dog being so friendly to you?" said Isabella.

"Teddy likes the sound of our instruments. And he knows that we made the plants stop their attack."

"Do I know you?" said Isabella. "You look familiar. And how do you know the name of my dog?"

"I don't think that she recognizes us said Biff."

" Well, it has been 10 years." How do you expect her to recognize us?" said Scud.

"Wait, it can't be. Biff? Scud? But how are you so old? And why are you living in the jungle? I thought you would be in the castle, she said. "Boy, am I glad to see you two. We almost didn't make it," said Isabella.

"I'm glad we could return the favor. I have always wanted to help you after what you did for us, but I didn't think we would see you again," said Scud. This is our friend Magento. He's a faun.

"Hello Magento. Why are you living out in the jungle away from the other monsters?"

That is a long story," he said. Slowly, many children who were hiding now revealed themselves.

"How did all these children get here?" said Isabella.

"That is an even longer story," said Magento. "You should rest, and tonight, my friends will tell it."

That evening, they sat around the fire as they listened to Biff and Scud tell their tale. After they began their lives in Monsterville, they met Magento. He believed that the Leviathan would be back, and that as long as it was still alive, there would be a time of great unrest. He told them of the fauns who lived deep in the jungle and kept away from the rest of the creatures of Monsterville. They saw themselves as protectors of human boys and girls.

Biff and Scud also wanted to help children, and with the fauns' help, they began traveling to the human world to save those who were being mistreated by adults. They brought them to their camp and gave them a safe place to live and grow up. There was a whole colony of human children who wanted to start their lives over, and not live in fear. Now they lived in a peaceful place where they learned to love themselves and be loving to others.

"That is an amazing tale," said Sweet Pea. "But how did you both become older?"

I'm not exactly sure," said Biff. I know that Monsterville began changing. Objects would disappear and then reappear at different locations. The ground would shake, without warning, and then stop just as quickly as it had begun. We woke up one day to find that The Eastern Mountains were missing. Monsterville became so unstable, that an enormous wormhole opened in the middle of the jungle and engulfed us. When we reappeared, we were older. "

"Wow!" said Isabella. I can't believe how you've both changed. Teddy notices it too, it's just not your flutes. He really likes you both. Hey, will you go with us to see the diamond troll? We need to solve this mystery of nothingness, and we could use your help?

"Thanks for asking us," said Biff, "but the children need our help." Biff then turned to Sweet Pea. "If it is okay with you my great one, we would like to stay here and continue our work."

"Yes, you should stay and help the humans," said Sweet Pea. "Besides, it's the savior who needs to speak to the diamond troll."

"We will be with you in spirit," said Scud.

As they approached the mountain, the little king finished one of his favorite tales. "And that is the story of how the golden dwarf of Monsterbrook Hollow sprained his tuchus." he said.

"Thank you for that wonderful story Sweet Pea," said Isabella.

"...And schlepped it through the Valley of No Return."

"Do you think we can share more of the Golden Dwarf's adventures later? I am getting nervous about meeting this diamond troll," said Isabella.

"Sure. The Golden Dwarf had many wonderful adventures. I can't wait to tell you more of them. Well, we are almost there anyway. Did I mention you'll need to cross the bridge of the pure hearted if you want to speak to the diamond troll? " said Sweet Pea."

"You mean, we´ll need to cross, don't you?"

"No, I mean you'll have to cross. Without me!" said Sweet Pea.

"What? There is no way that I can do this on my own." said Isabella.

"You *can* do it," Sweet Pea said. Only the savior can cross the bridge. So it must be only you. "You saved our land once before; you can do it again. Also, there is a small detail about you being the one who willed me and this entire world into existence! Trust yourself!"

Then Isabella thought more about this. Monsterville needed her. If she didn't try, then the North Mountains might never return to Monsterville. And even worse, this world will continue to disappear. To make matters more difficult, Sweet Pea looked at Isabella with big glassy eyes and a curled bottom lip. She had a weakness for adorable pleading faces. She had to do this, if not for her, then for all Monsterkind.

"I'll do it," she said.

"That's fantastic," said Sweet Pea. I'll wait for you at the foot of the mountain." As he walked away, he said, "And by the way, no one has ever crossed the bridge and lived to tell about it. So be careful"

"What was that?" said Isabella, as she turned around.

"Be careful," said Sweet Pea, as his voice faded into the distance.

"No, what was the part before that?" said Isabella.

Sweet Pea's voice sounded fainter with every step he took. "I said no one has lived to tell about it. But don't worry about that. You can do it. You have the power of belief. You helped bring me back to life. You are the only one who can save us."

So Isabella started climin'
Surmounting rocks which did abound
And came upon a clearing,
thunderstruck without a sound
This wasn't, you know, a place to go
 And share it with your mommy,
For it was a lonely road, both dark and cold,
filled with the remains of monstrous bodies
choked up and raw from what she saw,
the savior started snotting
Yet in despair, she was still aware,
some monsters were still rotting
Many had tried to cross the chasm wide,
for weakness did they abhor
But they could not tame the roaring flames,
so their hearts beat nevermore
This all had beene a gruesome scene,
and she peeked at the putrescence
she was feeling kinda queasy
cause this rocked her very essence
The bridge had lain in front of her
just beyond the clearing's edge
The earth beneath was far from reach
as she looked over the ledge.

Then she noticed her shoes were sticky,

something had come upon them

her soles seemed truly icky,

finding flesh of carcasses on them

And the savior saw in the rock up high,

a sarcophagus on which had been inscribed:

What happens to a kasadea deferred?
Is it merely an idea in a case?
Yes, aloe vera soothes the skin
But of a broken monstrous race?
With skin scorched from fear's eruption?

Do you have that special somethin?
Are you the one who finds the gumption?
Not the type that clings to your shoe
But the kind that sticks despite your mood

"Gumption? Huh? More like dumption!" she said

and threw her shoes into the abyss. "And what does a

kasadea have to do with saving the world? I have

absolutely no idea. But I am feeling rather hungry."

Then she read the rest of the message

If you want to cross this chasm
you must have a heart that's pure
One that burns through the threshold's blaze
But none have made it heretofore

About to turn away, thoughts rose

upon the surface of her mind,

recalling what her father had said

whenever she was in a bind

¨You can move towards what you fear,

which will turn you against the tide

But to wield the power of belief,

you must have a heart, purified"

After all, she had made this world

 from her innermost desires

which dwarfed her fear, for the clearly near

flaming wooden bridge of fire

So she walked up to the edge

with anticipation of what awaited

And felt the singe of the burning flame

which still had not abated

She took a breath as she held

the thick rope still a burnin'

Having ignited the fuse of hope,

her mind had filled with yearning

Suddenly the fire stopped,

and the flames they did subside

As she walked across the blazing bridge

with a heart, purified

As she walked into a dense fog, she heard the faint sound of an acoustic guitar. She thought she could see an outline of what appeared to be Neil Diamond. But as she continued to move closer, she saw that it was just a troll who had an elongated nose with a wart on it. He was a short little fella, about 3 feet tall and brown who had on an ill-fitting wig of thick wavy black hair and who wore a glittering blue sequined tasseled shirt, the top open buttons exposing a rug of curly dark chest hair. And when he smiled, he had a golden tooth which sparkled in the light.

"Hi there," said Isabella."

"Hey Hayadooin" said the troll as he continued to strum his guitar. "Can I help you?"

"Excuse me, are you...?"

"Yeah, that's right. I'm Neil friggin Diamond the Troll. I wish I didn't have to stay here in the middle of nowhere, but hey, *what a you gonna do?*

Isabella just stared, speechless. The troll, starting to get uncomfortable, eventually said, "Hey, You gotta problem?"

"No mister. I'm just trying to find the wise one who can help me save this land." Are you the wise one I am looking for?" she said.

"Well, whoever told you that, "He don't know from nothin." Then Isabella's eyes began to well up. "Hey, little girl, what's with the long face?" Why so ferclempt?

"So you don't know how to save Monsterville?"

"Hey, don't yous friggin worry about what *you* think *I'm* supposed to know. Wait a sec. Yooze tellin me that *yooze* the one who crossed *that* bridge? Then he paused, looking her over. Yooze? Ovah heah? With the watery eyes? Whatsamattaferu? Not for nuttin' but, you are *too* mousy to make it to *this* side of *that* bridge. Jees, what's this world comin to?"

"Okay Mr. Troll...

"Mr. Diamond the Troll," he said.

"Yes, sorry, Mr. Diamond the Troll. Please tell me how I can save Monsterville from vanishing?"

"You're giving me agita ovah heah. Okay, okay, I'll tell you what to do. I got a note from a guy. It has the answers you seek. What yooze lookin' at me for kid? Go see where you gotta go." Then the diamond troll gave her the parchment, and Isabella began to read it.

Just as every chicken has hatched from an egg
And every tripod must have a third leg
As moss depends on the stillness of a stone
As the absence of others makes us alone
And a lion needs the wild to roam

Just as every canyon has its hole.
And every bridge has its troll,
Just as every toenail needs a toe,
Every belief needs someplace to go

When you put lox on a bagel, a gap is filled
When you look at a map, a route is revealed.
Just as every leaf comes from a tree
Every drop of water wants to return to the sea.

To find the answer to your enigma
Look deep inside yourself, now see ya.

And if this don't help yous, Hey, fugetaboutit. Now get
outta heah kid"

From Yours Truly

After she read the note, she said to herself, "Well, that was completely unhelpful. It was just a bunch of fortune cookies put together. And I wasted my time with a troll who thinks he's Neil Diamond." Then she noticed that the Eastern Mountains were still missing. "How can this be? I created this world because I believed it. So if I believe these mountains should be here, why aren't they?"

Then she thought back to when she was a scared little girl and when her dad tried to console her." There is no such thing as monsters," he had said. She heard her dad's voice repeating in her mind. Then she realized that her dad's lack of faith is what has been making Monsterville vanish.

"I am not the only one that has this power. My dad must have it too." She knew what she must do, convince her dad that Monsterville is real. "That is what the diamond troll meant when he said the answer is deep inside of me. Now it's time for me to go and leave this diamond troll," she said to herself. And before she left, she shouted, "Shine on, you crazy diamond."

Horatio de la Fleur had inherited the house from his fourth cousin, Harlow Hubris Hornswiffle. Hornswiffle had fancied himself as both decorator and taxidermist, which explained why Horatio, who should have been writing his novel, found himself staring at an impeccably dressed stuffed platypus propped up next to a potted geranium. He was both fascinated and horrified by the room's decor. A snarling groundhog head was mounted on the wall. And an adorable micro poodle with a gold-plated name tag that read Fluffkins stood on a trophy for best in show, donning a leather motorcycle jacket as she stood suspended on her hind legs in a perpetual doggie treat begging position.

But what really disturbed him was the stuffed abomination propped on his desk alongside his typewriter -a hedgehog on all fours tensed up and showing its teeth. He had an eerie feeling about that hedgehog, and as he typed away at his desk, lost in thought about the characters in his book, he would look to his left, having forgotten that the creature was next to him, and seeing a wide-open mouth filled with pointy teeth, suddenly let out a shriek of fear. "That's it. I don't care how much Harlow loved you. You've got to go!" he said to himself. But as he attempted to move it away, he cried out, "Doh!" when his hand was caught by the sharp prickers. So he rolled up a newspaper and pushed the animal into a box and placed it in the closet. Then noticing he was bleeding from what he would later refer to as the ghastly hedgehog incident, he wrapped his hand with his handkerchief and once again began punching the keys on his antique underwood typewriter.

The wall directly across from the desk had an enormous golden framed Renaissance style portrait of the man responsible for this decor, donning a pencil styled mustache. The portrait eerily overlooked the now stuffed Fluffkins who was arranged in such a way, that she looked as if she were begging for a treat. "That Hornswiffle was one weird dude," Horatio said to himself. He wore thick black framed glasses, and as he typed the intermittent clickety clacks echoed throughout the study. He looked up and suddenly had the strange feeling that Hornswiffle had been watching, not to mention those stuffed animals were starting to freak him out. So he rounded them up and put them in the closet. "I must be getting paranoid," he said to himself. Then he went back to his seat, looked at Harlow Hornswiffle, and once again banged away at his typewriter. Clickety clack, click clackity clack. Horatio was becoming quite tired as he listened to the rhythmic sound from the typewriter keys. As he struggled to keep his eyes open, he thought he heard a voice. He shook his head and continued typing. "I must have been dreaming," he said to himself, for he knew what he had heard was too incredible to be considered. The whispering continued, telling him to pick up his pen and open one of the old books on the shelf.

The general decor of the house was grueling. Among the most visually offensive was the bathroom connected to the study, with pea green floral wallpaper and the mauve sink and toilet. The house needed updating, and the whole thing was such an enormous undertaking, Horatio thought it was best to leave things the way they were. As he sat on his mauve toilet wearing his bathrobe and fuzzy bunny slippers, he looked at the decor and said to himself, "Harlow, you had the strangest taste." Then, he could hear a faint voice whispering to him. Suddenly, Horatio's eyes started to roll back, and picking up the magazine on the floor, began to frantically scribble on the back cover. Then his wife knocked on the door. "Are you okay dear?" Horatio snapped out of it. "Of course I am." I must have fallen asleep is all. I'll be out in a minute." He thought he had begun to lose his mind. "The eyes of Harlow were memorizing, and when he was in the study, Horatio felt as if Harlow could see right into his soul.

Some time had passed, and Horatio would often spend hours in his study. As he typed away at his desk he would often feel drowsy. This night was no exception. He stopped, and slowly took his fingers off the keys, staring at the soft light coming through the window from the brightness of the full moon. Then, as his eyes began to roll back, he made a low continuous humming sound. When he opened his desk drawer, his movement was mechanical, as if he were controlled by a force that was not his own. He opened the drawer without looking down and took out a large dusty book which he placed on his desk. As he flipped through the pages, he saw highly detailed and colorful illustrations of scenes along with words penned in a gothic style.

The first image was of Isabella in a nightgown as a little girl, terrified from a sharp toothed monster which hissed at her in her room. Then he turned the page and there was an illustration of her blowing away the tiny monster in her hand, then there was a picture with a red sky, black debris in the air, and erupting volcanoes. The next page was of a creature with golden fur who was wearing a vest, looking up at the sun on a beautiful day while he was in a meadow of lush green grass. And as he turned the pages, he saw his daughter swinging a sword at a large slithering beast. Then a cute furry golden monster on a mountain top was talking to a troll. On an empty page Horatio de la Fleur began sketching a picture of himself, with his eyes rolled back, at the very desk where he now sat., as the full moon cast a faint purplish light through the window. He then turned the page and started drawing what looked like a wormhole.

Suddenly, the middle of the wormhole began to move. It spun faster as it increased in size, taking on a golden hue as the inside went downward, becoming thinner at the bottom as if one were looking down from the top of a tornado. Objects on the desk were pulled towards it as papers began flying around the room. Horatio was still entranced, and by this time his mumbling had become quite loud.

Suddenly an enormous scaly talon reached up from the wormhole and grabbed Horatio's neck. He immediately opened his eyes and in complete shock, screamed as the beast pulled him through.

Narrator:

Horatio's jaw clenched, and his muscles tightened
He was more than a little bit frightened
As he and the creature had plummeted toward the
ground
And as that Leviathan did dive from the sky
Horatio was way too scared to cry
He was so fearful he couldn't even make a sound

In the crushing grip of the creature's talon
Isabella's dad did end up wailin'
Caught by the beast ready to do all sorts of wrong
Now a wave of flame had engulfed the land
There was nothing now which he could demand
And he was a prayin' and a wishin' that he'd never
even been born

And as for hope, he thought there was none
As the beast flew him up towards the sun
A sky of blue changed to a bloody sea of red
From its flaming mouth a fire churned
Horatio didn't know if he'd be burned
And was wonderin' if he was gonna to be eaten or left
for dead

Now moving with the beast on this hellish ride

were eels with wings which flew alongside

These creatures were at once fantastical and mean

The beast had a loud forceful voice

Horatio listened cause he had no choice

It was the most strangest thing you happened to ever

did see

Winged Eels:

My liege gonna make you cry right now.

Leviathan:

I'm gonna make your will bow!

Winged Eels:

Not for nothin but you're

Leviathan and Winged Eels:

Not allowed

Leviathan:

To escape my death grip kung fu

Leviathan and Winged Eels:

Pow!

Winged Eels:

Pow! Right now!

Horatio:

I barely know what I could say.

My disbelief you did betray.

I wish you'd put me down, come what may.

Now all I can do is close my eyes and

Ensemble:

Pray.

Horatio:

That's it. (Raising up his palms and shrugging in hopelessess)

Leviathan:

Your fear's gonna change this whole

Leviathan and Winged Eels:

Town.

Leviathan:

 Adding molten lava which makes the

Leviathan and Winged Eels:

Rounds.

Winged Eels:

You can't touch these awesome sounds,

Leviathan:

Making Superman lose by leaps and

Leviathan and Winged Eels:

Bounds.

Narrator:

Then the beast dropped the girl's dad on the beach
It flew up in the sky but was still within reach
soarin' way up high, then swoopin' down breathin' fire,
Horatio kept away from the burnin' flame
hidin' behind some rocks which had remained
He pleaded for help, 'cause his situation was quite dire

Then the Leviathan circled back down below
He came towards me, but why? I don't know
Fearful and worried I certainly did seem
Now I'm running away from this hulking beast
Help, help, I'm almost within its reach
I don't think I even have time to scream
"Hey, I'm tellin' a story ovah heah! Aaaah!"
(Suddenly the Leviathan breathes fire on the narrator burning him to a crisp. Then a little monster gets off

112

his folding chair. Next to him is a megaphone that says DIRECTOR. He is wearing a beret, mustache, circular glasses, and a black turtleneck. The director yells at the Leviathan through a megaphone)

Director:

Cut! No, No, No! You are not supposed to kill the narrator. Now I'll have to get Gerald to do it. Come Gerald. Aaaah!

(Gerald puts down his mop, and then is reluctantly pushed into the narrator's place and handed the script. But the Leviathan burns the director to a crisp too).

Gerald:

(Frantically trying to read through the scene quickly points to Isabella's dad.)

Hey, you down there! Whatsa matta with you? Go ahead and read your lines already, an keep this loose nut with wings offa me!

Horatio:

This all raises some serious questions.

Gerald:

Just get back to doin' ya thang little man! Besides, you got company. Take 2, Scene 39.

(Clapping the director's clapboard and pointing to the Leviathan who is circling back and closing in on Isabella's dad.)

Horatio:

I'm gonna hide and not make a sound
I'll get lost, and won't be found
Please don't eat me, I'm not proud
I feel a storm comin' on, through my pelvic

Ensemble:

Cloud. (*Pointing and looking down at his pelvis*)

Horatio:

That's right, I'm gonna make in my pants.

Gerald:

(*Reading from the script*)
In the study, the girl, dog, and monster arrived,
shocked at what they saw with their very own eyes
Books and papers were scattered all over the floor
The desk was turned over and glass had shattered
And they were worried that her dear old dad had been
battered
They wanted to save him before he got hurt any more

A large book laid there from what I am told
It was embroidered with 24 Karats of gold
And Monsterville was what it happened to be called
the book could no longer be ignored

For time was something they could not afford
And it was the most bizarre thing in the whole, whole
wide world

The girl could not believe what that book did reveal
A picture of her dad dragged into Monsterville
As she flipped the page, it changed to a harsh fiery
land.
Then Sweet Pea stomped on the soft pine floor
creating a wormhole, which was a big ol' door
They jumped through the portal, Bella with the book in
hand

Horatio saw a swirling light appear
And he didn't want to be too near
So he stayed behind those rocks, wanting to save his
hide
Sweet Pea and Isabella were now in this land
jumping up and down on hot pebbles and sand
Their raison d'etre would not fail to be denied
(Gerald points to the script and shrugs his shoulders)
Hey, what am I, a Shakespeare ohva heah?

Horatio:

Bells we must escape from this

Ensemble:

Thing.

Horatio:

I don't know where you have

Ensemble:

Been.

Horatio:

My heart's got beats, my head's got

Ensemble:

Rings.

Horatio:

I now believe, what you've been

Ensemble:

Seein'.

Isabella:

Don't begin to burst at the seams.

Sweet Pea:

This beast is real even in your dreams.

Isabella:

It thrives on fear.

Sweet Pea:

And on your screams.

Isabella:

But we need not flee this obscene

Sweet Pea and Isabella:

Scene.

Isabella:

I don't have time to explain.

Sweet Pea:

I know this whole thing seems insane.

Isabella:
I'm like Indiana Jones.

Sweet Pea:
And I'm like David Blaine. Let's help this world to
ENSEMBLE:
Remain.

GERALD
Isabella vowed her dad would not be forsaken
She was all shook up by whom that monster had taken
And she shouted, "Give him back!" Oh how she was
mad
Then Sweet Pea said, "You must be brave and strong,
if you intend to right this wrong
And take away all the fear your dad ever had"

Then they saw him run to a hill up high
while the beast kept swooping down from the sky
sharp talons outstretched, wanting to see him bleed
Isabella shouted out to her dear ol' dad
who could be a modern-day Sir Galahad
"Be brave in your heart, in your thoughts, and in your
deeds"

"Dad," she said. "You need to believe the beast can't hurt you."

"Monster, you can't harm me," he said rather weakly. But the Leviathan let out a cantankerous roar with massive teeth dripping with mucus and blood which left her dad shaking in fear.

Then Isabella shouted, "You have nothing to be scared of. You're afraid because you believe this beast is real.

"Of course it's real. Look at this mucus on me."

"Dad, remember what you taught me when I was a little girl! You taught me how to face my fears. Just believe that it can't hurt you, and it will go away."

Standing firmly, her dad said, "Monster be gone," as he held up the storybook in front of him. The Leviathan flew directly toward her dad, with its jaw open and teeth exposed, about to clamp down onto his chest, and drag him against the ground. Then it sniffed its nose as it approached, slowly, menacingly.

"I can smell your fear," said the beast. "I remember that same smell when you were a little boy, whimpering under your blanket, as you heard your mother each night crying for help, pleading for you to protect her. Yes, I was there. You helped me grow. A part of you always knew I was there listening. A part of you has always known I am real. I kept your secret. Isn't that right little Horatio? Now I have a secret for you to keep," he said, slithering closer as he spoke. The steam from the beast's breath came out as it whispered, "Now I'm coming...for...you." Her dad could take no more. He ran away, having become the scared little boy from his childhood. The beast leaped into the air and then landed right in front of him, and the slithering eels wrapped their slimy bodies around each of his limbs. And in the distance where the Eastern Mountains formerly stood, there was now a volcano, and it began to thunder and rain blood.

As the Leviathan exposed its teeth in its drooling mouth and Horatio stood transfixed, shaking with fear, a large glob of mud landed on the side of the Leviathan's face. It wiped the wet muddy soil from its eyes and when it turned to see where it had come from, standing before it were all the creatures of Monsterville led by Tyranno-trumposaurus. Then the beast was pelted with a barrage of moist mud pies which landed in its mouth, on its nose, and in its eye. "There's mud in your eye, ya schmendrick," said the Tyranno-trumposaurus . "I hath besmudgen you."

Then the voices from the crowd chanted, "Yeah, we don't want your steaming mud pies." And Scud and Biff were there too, hurling mud patties. Then the beast attacked the crowd, seriously injuring Smelliosis and a few others. Scud and Biff were brave, and attacked with their swords, but the beast's tail knocked them both down. Seeing Isabella's dad in the distance, the Leviathan flew towards him filled with rage.

Tyranno-trumposaurus came out of the monstrous crowd, ripped the vampire squid from its head revealing its baldness, and said, "I destroy you in the name of justice." Then, using his tiny hands, he hurled the squid onto the beast's face, which jammed its vampiric blood funnel through the beast's nose. But the beast just ripped the squid off its face, and devoured it, gulping it down its plated food gullet. Isabella was knocked down and the beast gloated.

"I have won. Now I'm going to kill your dad and make you watch as I melt his cowardly flesh off his body. "Where is your belief now Savior?" Isabella had become afraid once again. Then suddenly, a blade glistening with blood protruded from the beast's chest. As the beast fell to the ground, behind it stood Horatio de la Fleur with the bloody saber in his hand.

Horatio then opened the book to the final page, and an energy center suddenly revealed itself. It swirled slowly, becoming larger, and it began to pull the beast toward it. It screeched as it struggled to fly away. But

Horatio kept saying, "Be gone," each time more forcefully, using every fiber of his will. And with each phrase, the creature was pulled toward the vortex, and became smaller as its claws dug into the earth. Then it was absorbed into the book, which her dad held up, and he quickly snapped it shut.

The king called all monsters for a meeting,

Some were bleeding and all were needing

The Monster Pappy, who would now be leading

He said, "Monsters, we cannot be defeated

We have imprisoned the Leviathan

He must think again about who he is and

his capture was sorely needed

Let us all sing a heartfelt chorus,

in acceptance of this new world

bestowing an honorable title

on this heroic and brave little girl

All of the sudden a tune did play

A sound from the crowd came, Barf Fader, carousing,

espousing, acceptance and love

which became the new monster way

As the boogeyman skulked in the shadows

Hocking a loogie onto the ground,

he saw a moist brightly hued egg of mucus,

which was as stunning as it was profound

It looked like a green lightsaber

with the outline of a body,

and Barf was reminded of Puke

his beloved yet estranged progeny

Thinking that little guy was in the sand,

he used the force and bent down,

lending that tiny jedi a hand

Barf then gave the monsters one more surprise

He raised his son, who became much larger

before everyone's tear filled eyes

Barf, turning to him said," I am your father,"

but that steaming Puke had replied,

"Thanks for the hand dad, but is it really an honor?"

Suddenly, out came the piano

And Puke Skycrawler began to sing

Barf Fader helped with the beautiful tune

for the newly anointed monster king

In a world that used to be derisory

Now they played Ebony and Ivory[1]

But using humanity and monstrosity

The words still had the same grandiosity

Each piano key was alive

Having an eye which was googly

and a teeny mouth which opened wide

and which sung quite beautifully

The monsters listened intently,

as the duo began to sing,

transfixed by the sweet melody

and happy for their wondrous king,

The piano keys had loosened

now comfortable with the groovy tune

blossoming before all the monsters
smooching their lips, sending kisses to the moon
the werewolf swayed to the music
 as he looked in the mirror,
combing his luscious chest hair and no longer
letting his fear of himself simmer
The zombie hugged the zombie slayer
and put his heart back in his chest
while Dr. Frankenstein's creature,
being overjoyed, called it a lovefest
The skeleton plucked his ribs
 to enhance the melody
filled with pride about the course
of Monsterville's love directed destiny
Of course Sweet Pea and Isabella hugged
 and held hands as the music played,
for there was no more evil
to taint the new monster way
The little king was grateful
that he now had his own special friend,
and he knew a happy head begins
after a heavy heart to mend
Once again, the passageway opened
Matter mysteriously unwoven,
so they could return to the world of men
The savior of this land entered the portal

with her dad by her side, both mere mortals
Having the hearts of all monster kind mended,
their journey to that foreign land had ended
And so concludes our epic saga,
of a special girl and a tiny monster

1. Known affectionately as Norma by giants throughout Monsterville, she is a creature which stands 15 feet tall, has pointy teeth, red beady eyes, and has been rumored to lay an occasional reptilian shelled egg. She likes carrots but will eat the furniture if it deems itself hangry enough.

2. Squirrelonomous: It enjoys throwing its nuts when it becomes excited, and for this reason is comparable with the **Tyranno-trumposaurus**

3. Tyranno-trumposaurus: Very similar to a Tyrannosaurus, in the sense that it is a monstrous predator with an enormous mouth, always roaring loudly, yet extremely small hands as compared to the rest of his body. It is always orange, for it knows not what it means to hide, as its survival depends on being seen. and can often be found in the wild grasping an unconsenting pussycat as it goes about its day, while its squid-like tentacled hair plugs flap in the wind.

Chapter 23 Notes

1. I almost put this stanza in. It has a different
    rhythm to it which I love. But how could I get rid
    of   Inigo Montoya?

    I'm like Robin Hood but more yeah
    a smooth swashbucklin destroya (de-stoy-yeah)

2. I love the Flash Gordon line, but this one is too
    good to vanish into the abyss. Thus, I included it in
    the notes.

    I'm the maestro to your moms
    And she's playing the organ,
    She's got her fingers on my chords,
    till 4 in the mornin

Chapter 24 Notes

1. Clownicula is a vampire clown with sharp
    elongated eye teeth and shiny oversized red shoes,
    orange cape over a black nightgown and curly
    locks of orange hair in hair rollers. He has a big
    round orange nose. He feeds on the color orange,
    leaving a putrid pea green in its place.

2.   Half skillet and half skeleton, and in an intimate
      relationship with spatul-fang-gorea, he is at once,
      creator of cuisine and decayer of flesh.

3.   A favorite delicacy of carnivorous and omnivorous
      monsters, particularly those who like to devour
      the cute and fluffy. It is essentially a frozen
      squirrel on a stick.

4.   At first, I had Pokey watch and Gumby swallow,
      but I opted for the allusion to Humpty Dumpty.
      Both have their merits.

Chapter 35 Notes

1.   I also thought Together Forever by Rick Astley
      would set the mood for this scene.

Other Books by Corey Wolff

The Journey of an Acorn

Mikey McMonsterson Goes to School